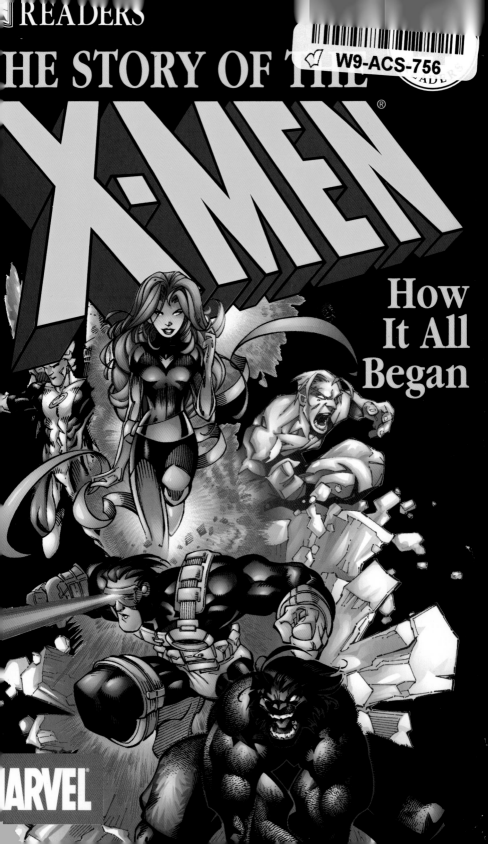

READERS

HE STORY OF THE

X·MEN

How
It All
Began

MARVEL

DK READERS

Level 3

Level 4

A Note to Parents and Teachers

The DK READERS series is a compelling reading program, designed in conjunction with leading literacy experts, including Dr. Linda Gambrell, Director of the Eugenge T. Moore School of Education at Clemson University. Dr Gambrell has served on the Board of Directors of the International Reading Association and as President of the National Reading Conference.

The series combines a highly visual approach with engaging, easy-to-read text. Each DK READER is guaranteed to capture a child's interest while developing his or her reading skills, general knowledge, and love of reading.

The four levels of DK READERS are aimed at different reading abilities, enabling you to choose the books that are exactly right for your children:

Level 1—Beginning to Read
Level 2—Beginning to Read Alone
Level 3—Reading Alone
Level 4—Proficient Readers

The "normal" age at which a child begins to read can be anywhere from three to eight years old, so these levels are intended only as a general guideline.

No matter which level you select, you can be sure that you are helping your child learn to read, then read to learn!

DK

LONDON, NEW YORK, DELHI,
MUNICH, AND MELBOURNE

Produced by
Shoreline Publishing Group
Editorial Director James Buckley, Jr.
Art Director Thomas J. Carling
Project Editor Michael Teitelbaum
Designer Brandy Young

For Dorling Kindersley Publishing
Senior Editor Cynthia O'Neill
Senior Managing Art Editor Cathy Tincknell
DTP Designer Andrew O'Brien
Production Nicola Torode
US Editor Gary Werner

Reading Consultant Linda Gambrell PhD

First American Edition, 2000

07 08 09 10 9 8

Published in the United States by
Dorling Kindersley Publishing, Inc.
375 Hudson Street, New York, New York 10014

ISBN-13: 978-0-7894-6697-6 (pb)
ISBN-13: 978-0-7894-6696-1 (hb)

Library of Congress Cataloguing-in-Publication Data

Teitelbaum, Michael.
The story of the X-men: how it all began/ by Michael Teitelbaum.
--1st American ed.
p. cm. -- (Dorling Kindersley readers)
ISBN 0-7894-6696-1 – ISBN 0-7894-6697-X (pbk.)
1. X-men (Comic strip) -- Juvenile literature. [1. X-men (Comic strip)
2. X-Men (Fictitious characters) 3. Cartoons and comics -- History and
criticism] I. Title. II Series.

PN6728.X2 T457 2000
741.5'973--dc21
00-034055

Printed and bound in China by L Rex Printing Co., Ltd.

Photography credits:
t=top, b=below, l=left, r=right, c=center,
AP/Wide World: 23tr, 38tl

Discover more at
www.dk.com

Contents

PROFICIENT
4
READERS

THE STORY OF THE
X-MEN
HOW IT ALL BEGAN

Written by Michael Teitelbaum

DK Publishing, Inc.

A new kind of hero

In 1963, the X-Men burst onto the comic book scene. The X-Men, who had been created by writer Stan Lee and artist Jack Kirby, were not a typical team of Super Heroes.

Since 1963, th have been mo than 25 differ X-Men series published.

The X-Men were teenagers. They *looked* human, for the most part, but were very different.

These teenagers were mutants. Their genetic makeup gave each one a special power. Most of the X-Men discovered that they had these incredible abilities at a young age. Many couldn't control their powers. Some were frightened by their unique skills.

It took one man, a mutant himself, to bring these talented young people together. He assembled them and taught them to control their powers. Then he shaped them into a team.

Today, the X-Men are stars of thousands of comic book adventures. They have appeared in popular television shows, as well as a Hollywood movie. But who are they? And how did this spectacular story begin?

The big screen
In the summer of 2000, the X-Men starred in their first feature film.

The first
The cover of the first X-Men comic book, published in September 1963.

Professor X has been confined to a wheelchair since an alien named Lucifer dropped a stone block on his legs. This was in revenge after the professor stopped Lucifer's race from invading Earth.

Wheels
Since losing the ability to walk, Professor X gets around in a special wheelchair. Noted actor Patrick Stewart played the part of Professor X in the X-Men's big screen debut.

Professor X

Professor Charles Xavier is the man responsible for bringing together the X-Men. He is known to his students as Professor X. Xavier is a mutant himself, and he possesses amazing mental powers.

Professor X is a telepath. This means that he can read minds or send messages into the minds of others. His mental powers also allow him to create illusions in other people's minds. He can make them believe they are seeing things that aren't really there.

Professor X can use his mental powers to temporarily paralyze people, so that they cannot move. He can wipe out specific memories, or cause complete amnesia, taking someone's memory away altogether.

The professor can even send out powerful mental bolts that knock a person unconscious.

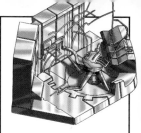

The professor also practices "astral projection." This means that he can send his mind traveling over great distances, while his body remains at home. Being a powerful telepathic mutant, Professor X also has the ability to sense other superhuman mutants at close range.

Super computer
Cerebro is Professor X's amazing computer. It is a "mutant tracking device," which allows the professor to reach out to other mutants anywhere in the world.

Online
Today, we can all reach out to communicate with others around the world, thanks to the internet!

Gene pool
Our bodies contain a genetic material called DNA (*below*). It is a kind of chemical code that makes us who we are. Mutants have special DNA, which gives them their powers.

On the team
Wolverine is one of the new characters who have joined the X-Men team over the years.

Mutants may look like humans, but they are quite different. Each one has some genetic difference that gives him or her a special power.

For years mutants have lived among humans, trying to get along with them. But due to human fear, ignorance, and prejudice, mutants have been made to suffer. They are treated like outsiders or freaks, and are feared and shunned.

Professor X's dream is to change this. He believes that mutants and humans should be able to live together in peace.

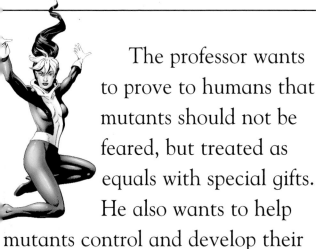

The professor wants to prove to humans that mutants should not be feared, but treated as equals with special gifts. He also wants to help mutants control and develop their special powers to help humanity.

To make this dream come true, Professor X set up a School for Gifted Youngsters. He used his family's mansion as the home base for his school. Over the years, many mutants have come to the school to study with the professor.

Touch sensitive
Rogue (*left*) joined the X-Men after she asked Professor X for help with her uncontrollable powers. She is able to absorb the memory and powers of anyone she touches—even her fellow X-Men!

Weather girl
Storm has also joined the original X-Men team since it was first set up. She possesses the incredible mutant ability to control weather conditions.

Early loss
Charles Xavier's father was a nuclear scientist. He was killed in an explosion while his son was still young.

Unstoppable
Cain Marko was serving as a soldier in Korea, when he found a mystical ruby in a lost temple. The gem transformed him into the evil Juggernaut.

"I'LL NEVER FORGET THAT FATEFUL HOLOCAUS ...FOR MY *FATHER* WAS KILLED IN THE BLAST:

...AND SO WE COMMIT BRIAN XAVIER TO THE EARTH!

IF ONLY *DAD* HAD BEEN ABLE TO ESCAPE THE BLAST...THE WAY *DR. MARKO* DID!

Professor X's own life didn't get off to an easy start. His father died when Charles was still a boy. His mother then married her husband's former colleague, Dr. Karl Marko. Charles's older stepbrother, Cain, always bullied young Charles and treated him cruelly.

Cain Marko would go on to become the being known as Juggernaut, one of the X-Men's greatest enemies.

Charles discovered his telepathy when he was still a boy. As he grew, he learned to control his powers.

He studied at Oxford University in England. After college, he spent time traveling, both in and out of the army. He saw Asia, then Israel. In Israel, he became friends with a man named Erik Magnus Lehnsherr.

Years later, Lehnsherr would become Magneto, the X-Men's greatest enemy.

Charles Xavier had a difficult childhood.

Shadow King
During a visit to Egypt, Professor X battled with Amahl Farouk, the Shadow King. Farouk was the first evil mutant the professor had ever met. After this, Professor X decided to spend his life protecting humans from evil mutants. He also vowed to protect innocent mutants from human oppression.

Professor X's first student was an eleven-year-old mutant, named Jean Grey, who also had great mental powers. Jean had been hurt by her own abilities, and was sent to the professor for treatment. He helped her recover, then taught her how to use her powers.

The team grows
Many mutants have joined the X-Men over the years, such as Banshee, whose voice can carry him through the air, and Colossus, who has superhuman strength.

Several years later, Professor X started his School for Gifted Youngsters. It contained a special training room, called the Danger Room. There, students could practice their mutant powers.

The Danger Room created training situations for students to deal with, using the special skills and techniques that the professor taught.

Using his mutant tracking device, Cerebro, Professor X searched the world. He found five young mutants to train.

The X-Men were born!

The originals
The first group of students at the School for Gifted Youngsters were Cyclops, Iceman, Marvel Girl, Beast, and Angel.

On the move
Professor X rescued Nightcrawler as an angry mob was about to attack him. This X-Man has the ability to teleport himself from place to place.

Professor X explained their mission. "Some mutants wish to destroy the human race," he told them. "It is our job to protect humankind from evil mutants."

Cyclops takes his name from the Cyclopes, a race of one-eyed giants from ancient Greek mythology. These huge monsters sometimes trapped unfortunate sailors who landed on their island. Very few ever survived to see their home again.

Cyclops

Scott Summers' father was a test pilot in the US Air Force. While flying his family back from a vacation, their plane was attacked by alien invaders. Scott's mother gave him and his brother the only parachute on the plane. She then pushed the boys out of the plane.

The plane crashed, but the young boys survived. They hit the ground hard, and Scott suffered a head injury. He remained in a coma for a year.

In his mid-teens, Scott experienced terrible headaches and eyestrain. Then, one day, while in New York City, his mutant power erupted. Powerful beams of force, called "optic blasts," shot uncontrollably from his eyes.

Illustration by Howard Bender

The optic blasts slammed into a crane at a construction site. Pieces of the crane hurtled toward the terrified crowd below.

Scott used his optic blasts again to destroy the falling metal chunks before anyone in the crowd got hurt.

Although he had saved many lives, the crowd blamed Scott for the accident. He became a fugitive.

Glass wear
Cyclops cannot shut off his optic blasts at will. He must wear a special visor or glasses with lenses that block the beams.

MUST ACT --NOW!!

Safety shield
The ruby quartz in Cyclops' special glasses works in the same way as the lead shield you wear at the dentist. This protects you from the invisible, but harmful, x-rays your dentist uses to check for cavities in your teeth.

Due to his childhood head injury Scott could not control his optic blasts. An eye doctor made him special glasses with ruby quartz lenses. Scott's deadly eye beams could not pass through them.

Scott was frightened of his newfound power. He was afraid he might accidentally hurt someone.

Professor X met Scott when he rescued him from an evil mutant called the Living Diamond.

THOUGH HE'S ONE SUPERHERO WHO WOULD RATHER *SWITCH OFF* HIS SUPER POWER THAN *FIGHT*, THE SENSATIONAL MR. SUMMERS JUST *CAN'T HELP* POSSESSING ENOUGH MIND-STAGGERING MIGHT TO DEMOLISH A FULLY-ARMORED *TANK*...

THUS, A FEW MOMENTS LATER...

..THEN, YOU INTEND TO FORM A GROUP OF *MUTANTS*--EACH WITH SOME EXTRAORDINARY *POWER*--

--AND YOU WANT ME TO BE THE *FIRST MEMBER?*

PRECISELY! YOU WILL BE THE *NUCLEUS* --AROUND WHICH I SHALL *BUILD* THE GROUP!

WELL--WHAT DO YOU *SAY?* ARE YOU *WITH* ME, LAD?

YOU KNOW IT... SIR!

He asked Scott to join his new team, the X-Men. Scott agreed and became the first mutant to join the X-Men, taking the name Cyclops.

Cyclops' skills developed quickly. He learned to fire his optic blasts with pinpoint accuracy and enough power to shatter a steel door.

Once the original five X-Men had all been recruited, Cyclops became Professor X's trusted second-in-command.

Idealist
When the professor promised to teach Scott how to use his power to help humans and mutants, he was appealing to Scott's idealism.

Brave in battle
In addition to using his powerful optic blasts, Cyclops is also a brilliant battle strategist and an expert in hand-to-hand combat. And, like all the X-Men, Cyclops sharpens both his mutant skills and his combat skills in the Danger Room.

Slow down
Why does
water freeze?
When the
temperature
drops below
32°F (0°C),
the water
molecules slow
down until the
liquid becomes
a solid.

Baby Bobby
Bobby Drake
was the
youngest of the
original X-Men.
He grew in
maturity during
his time with
the team.

Iceman

Bobby Drake has the mutant power
to create ice. He discovered this
astonishing ability while he was in
his early teens, but kept it a secret.
Then, one night, fate stepped in and
changed Bobby's life forever.

 While Bobby was on a date with
his girlfriend, a bully attacked the
couple. To save them both, Bobby
used his power to encase the bully
in a solid block of ice.

Bobby Drake was forced to reveal his
powers when he tackled a local bully.

When the townspeople heard about this, a mob came after Bobby, thinking that *he* was the real menace. The local sheriff took Bobby to jail for his own protection.

Professor X learned about these events and sent Cyclops, his only X-Man at the time, to recruit Bobby. But Bobby refused to go with him and used his ice power to battle Cyclops. Soon the angry antimutant mob threatened them both!

Iceman then... and now (below)

GET YOUR HANDS OFF, ;EEEEEEEEEE!

Slick skin
At first, Iceman looked like a walking snowman. His body was clumsy and rough. As he studied and gained more control of his powers, his body changed and his skin became as smooth as ice.

*Iceman, Beast,
and Angel in*
the new Defenders.

Protection
Iceman has the
ability to create
ice shields from
thin air. He
uses the shields
to protect
himself and his
fellow X-Men
from attack.

Professor X reached out with his incredible mental powers. He was able to stop the angry mob and take away their memory of Bobby's powers. Then Cyclops helped Bobby escape.

Bobby Drake was grateful for Professor X's help. He accepted his offer to join the X-Men. He agreed to study with the professor to learn to control and expand his powers, and he took the name Iceman.

Soon Iceman learned to lower his body temperature, as well as the temperature in the air around him. He practiced projecting intense cold from his body onto any object. Sometimes he could lower the temperature to -105°F (-76°C).

Iceman also learned to freeze any moisture in the air into incredibly hard ice. He can shape this frozen moisture into ice slides, for superfast travel. He can also create ice shields, or ice grenades to fling at evil mutants.

Iceman can easily exist in subzero temperatures and can turn his body into a block of ice.

Despite these powers, Iceman only has the strength of a normal man of his age and build.

Surf's up! Iceman can ride the ice slides he creates like a surfer riding a frozen wave.

Marvel Girl

When she was ten years old, Jean Grey witnessed a tragedy that changed her entire life.

Jean's best friend, Annie, was killed in a car accident. Jean held her dying friend in her arms. The powerful emotions Jean experienced as Annie died activated Jean's hidden telepathic powers.

The horror of this experience caused Jean to become withdrawn and depressed. She was frightened of her newfound telepathic powers. She didn't know how to control them.

A year later, Jean's parents brought her to Professor X. He realized right away that the young girl possessed mutant powers and began treating her.

Professor X used his own telepathic ability to set up shields in Jean's mind. This stopped her from using her telepathic powers until she was old enough to control them. The professor did teach young Jean how to use her ability to move objects with her mind.

Mind power
Uri Geller became famous in the 1970s for using "mental powers" to bend spoons and move objects.

A few years later, Jean reached her mid-teens. Professor X came to see her. He asked her to join his new team of young mutants, the X-Men. The professor was training this group to use their powers to help humans and mutants alike.

Professor X promised to train Jean to use her mental powers. These were similar to his powers, though not as strong. She joined the team, taking the name Marvel Girl.

Professor X removed the shields he had put up when Jean was eleven. Marvel Girl was now ready to develop fully her own telepathic abilities.

Jean's skills grew. Soon, she could read minds and put her own thoughts into other people's minds.

Marvel Girl also learned to stun enemies with powerful mental bolts projected from her mind.

Her telekinetic powers improved. She could raise herself into the air. She learned to move objects, and even people, with her mind.

Name game
During her years with the X-Men, Jean Grey has been known by three different names: Jean Grey, Marvel Girl, and Phoenix.

Hank McCoy's father, Norton, worked at a nuclear power plant. There, he was exposed to massive amounts of radiation during an accident. Norton was unharmed, but the radiation affected his genes. As a result, Hank was born a mutant.

Beast

Thanks to his superhuman strength, agility, endurance, and speed, Hank McCoy was always a great athlete. He could run incredibly fast and for very long distances without getting tired. His strength was as great as that of 10 men. And he could climb and swing from tree branches better than the best gymnast.

As a teenager, these mutant powers allowed Hank to become a star football player. He was not an outcast, like many other mutants.

Eventually, his abilities brought him to the attention of both Professor X and a costumed criminal known as El Conquistador.

WELL *DONE,* YOUNG GLADIATOR! YOU HAVE EQUALED THE *BEST* OF MY TRUSTED MEN! BUT I HAVE *SPED* HERE TO DEMON-STRATE THAT --

--YOU ARE *NO* MATCH FOR-- *THE CONQUISTADOR!*

HUHHH?

El Conquistador captured Hank's parents and forced the young mutant to help in his evil schemes. But with the help of the X-Men, Hank defeated the criminal.

Professor X then invited Hank to join the X-Men. He agreed and became part of the original team. Because of his oversized hands and feet, Hank's X-Men code name was the Beast.

Huge hands
Unlike most mutants, Hank McCoy showed signs of his mutation right from birth. His hands and feet were unusually large! But Hank was able to use them to great effect.

As well as great physical powers, Beast has a brilliant mind, too! He became one of the world's leading experts in biochemistry and genetics. When he's not battling evil with his fellow X-Men, Beast can usually be found working on an experiment.

Smart guy
Studying with Professor X, Beast earned his Ph.D. in biochemistry. He is the most intellectual of the original X-Men.

Color change
Originally Beast's fur was gray. Now it's blue.

After he graduated from the School for Gifted Youngsters, Beast developed a special chemical formula. It helped bring out the hidden powers in mutants.

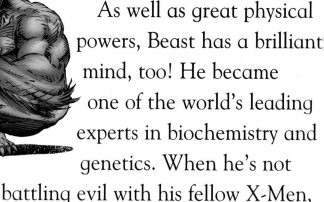

Beast drank the formula himself and went through an incredible change. Fur grew all over his body. His ears became larger and pointed. His teeth grew into fangs.

The formula increased his strength, agility, endurance, and speed. But he no longer looked human. Hank McCoy had truly become a Beast.

Still as smart and gentle as ever, this scary-looking mutant continues to do his research and battle evil mutants as a member of the X-Men.

Other teams In addition to being an original member of the X-Men, Beast has also been a member of the Super Hero teams the Avengers, the Defenders, and X-Factor I.

THE *CHEMICAL!* IT'LL CHANGE ME-- AND IN AN HOUR'S TIME, I CAN CHANGE *BACK* AGAIN, JUST BY TAKING *ANOTHER* DRINK AS AN *ANTIDOTE.*

DON'T KNOW WHAT WILL HAPPEN IF YOU *MUTATE A MUTANT*-- BUT I'VE GOT TO TAKE THE *CHANCE*--

--- *I'VE GOT TO!*

THAT WASN'T *PRECISELY* THE TRUTH, WAS IT, HANK McCOY?

YOU DIDN'T *HAVE* TO---

--- BUT THE NEWLY-DISCOVERED *EGO* WHICH NOW CONTROLLED YOU TOLD YOU *DIFFERENTLY...*

--AND YOU *TOOK* THE HORMONAL EXTRACT---

---AND YOU--- *CHANGED!*

Angel

Warren Worthington III had everything money could buy. He also had something that no amount of money in the world could purchase. While in his early teens, wings began to grow from Warren's shoulder blades.

Flight
Birds fly by flapping their wings up and down. That motion pushes air downward and to the rear, creating a lift and forward movement.

Secrecy
To hide his wings from the other students at school, Warren strapped them to his body and hid them under his clothes. The restraint was uncomfortable, but essential!

> THESE RESTRAINING BELTS OF MINE KEEP MY WINGS FROM BULGING UNDER MY SUIT, BUT AFTER A WHILE THEY FEEL LIKE I'M WEARING A *STRAIT-JACKET!*

Over the years, the look of Angel's costume changed. This is how he appeared in 1963.

Warren discovered that he could use these wings to fly. He practiced his flying in secrecy and came to enjoy his mutant ability. But he kept this genetic difference hidden from the other boys at his exclusive boarding school.

One night, a fire broke out in his dormitory. Many lives were at stake. Warren decided to use his flying power in front of others. He swooped from the sky and rescued his fellow students from the fire.

To keep his identity a secret, Warren wore a long blond wig and a nightshirt. To many people, he looked like an angel.

Teamwork
In addition to being an original member of the X-Men, Angel also belonged to the Super Hero teams X-Factor, the Defenders, the Champions, and the Horsemen of the Apocalypse.

31

After he finished school, Warren became a costumed crimefighter in New York City. He called himself the Avenging Angel.

In this way, he came to the attention of Professor X, who asked him to join the X-Men. Warren agreed and became one of the original mutants at the professor's school.

He used the code name Angel.

New name
Angel left the X-Men for a while, when Professor X recruited some new members. He later rejoined the team. This is how the character looked in the late 1960s.

Heavy metal
Angel has undergone many changes over the years. For a time, his feathered wings were replaced by metallic ones. He now takes the name Archangel.

GOOD! YOU AVOIDED THE SECOND OBSTACLE WITH SECONDS TO SPARE!

KLACK!

AHHH! NOW I'M GETTING WARMED UP!

Angel's wings have superhuman strength. In addition to carrying his body weight into the sky, they can support another 500 pounds.

The wings are fully feathered, like a bird's, and are very flexible. They fold tightly against his body. In fact, Angel's entire body is perfect for flying.

His bones are hollow, like a bird's, making him very light. His eyes are specially formed to stand up to the high winds he must deal with when flying. And his lungs can draw oxygen from the air at the very high altitudes at which he cruises, where breathable air grows very thin. This means that, with severe strain, Angel can fly at 29,000 feet, which is almost as high as a jet plane!

New heights
Angel usually flies below the height of the clouds, 6,500 ft, although he can reach 10,000 ft with a little effort.

This streamlined version of Archangel is how he looks today.

33

Protection
Magneto's helmet protects him from missiles. It also saves him from energy weapons and mental attacks.

Charged
A magnet is a piece of metal that attracts or repulses other pieces of metal.

Magneto

Not all mutants agree that humans and mutants should live together in peace. Some believe that mutants, because of their superior powers, should destroy humans and take over the Earth.

One such evil mutant goes by the name Magneto, Master of Magnetism. As a young man he used the name Eric Magnus Lehnsherr. Sometimes he just used the name Magnus.

In his early teens, during World War II, Lehnsherr was a prisoner in a Nazi concentration camp. This was where he learned how brutally human beings could treat those they considered different.

After the war, Magneto discovered his mutant power. He possessed the astounding ability to control magnetism!

He moved to Israel. There, he met Professor X many years before the professor formed the X-Men.

Brood of evil
Magneto soon discovered that he was not the only evil mutant who believed in mutant domination over humans. Assembling like-minded mutants, he formed the Brotherhood of Evil Mutants to challenge the X-Men.

Originals
The original members of the Brotherhood of Evil Mutants include Toad and Mastermind, plus Scarlet Witch and Quicksilver, who are both Magneto's children!

Ageless
Magneto now looks much younger than his true age, because Alpha, the Ultimate Mutant, restored his youth.

Evil robots
The X-Men are often attacked by giant robots called Sentinels (*below*), whose only purpose is to capture and destroy mutants!

Professor X and Magneto became friends. They spent many hours debating whether or not mutants should live peacefully with humans. The two men teamed up. They worked together using their mutant powers to defeat a high-tech terrorist organization known as HYDRA.

Shortly after this victory, they went their separate ways. Magneto's incredible power increased. Soon he could lift a 30,000 ton object into the air simply by concentrating his powers of magnetism on the object. He could assemble complex equipment in mid-air just by using his mind. He also learned to create psychic shields to protect him from telepathic attacks.

As Magneto's power increased, so did his belief that the only way to make sure that mutants would be safe from the oppression of humans would be to conquer the human race. He would then make himself leader of Earth.

The X-Men have battled Magneto time and again to see that this never happens!

Married
After World War II, Magneto married a woman named Magda. They had a daughter, Anya. When a mob prevented Magneto from rescuing Anya from a fire, he used his powers to destroy them. This terrified Magda, who left her husband. She died a short time later.

NOTHING CAN RESIST MY MATCHLESS *MAGNETIC POWER!* BY HARNESSING ONLY A *FRACTION* OF THE NATURAL MAGNETISM THAT IS MINE, I CAN RAISE THEIR ENTIRE *SCHOOL BUILDING,* ONLY TO SEND IT CRASHING DOWN IN *RUINS!*

3-2-1 blastoff
At the time that *X-Men* #1 came out (1963), the United States was engaged in a space race with the Soviet Union. Here, American astronaut John Glenn blasts off in his Mercury capsule, *Friendship 7.*

The first adventure

Here is the story of the first X-Men adventure, as it appeared in X-Men #1.

Deep inside a secret laboratory, Magneto stared at his viewscreen. On the screen was the image of a missile, ready for launching at the Cape Citadel missile base nearby.

"The moment is at hand," he muttered. "The human race no longer deserves to rule Earth. The day of the mutants is upon us!"

As the missile blasted off, Magneto concentrated his mutant power. He sent waves of magnetic energy surging toward the missile. The powerful magnetic energy slammed into the missile, sending it crashing into the ocean.

"How could this happen?" asked the base's general. "Nothing could get through our security measures!"

Over the next few days, Magneto used his mutant power to destroy five more missiles. He also attacked the missile base in other ways. Panic spread throughout the base.

BUT HERE, MILES FROM THE LAUNCHING SITE, I, THE MIRACULOUS *MAGNETO*, ALONE SHALL MAKE A MOCKERY OF THEIR GREATEST EFFORT!

11.

AHHH! I CAN FEEL THE IRRESISTABLE WAVES OF PURE MAGNETIC ENERGY SURGING FROM ME! NOW, BY EXERTING EVERY IOTA OF POWER, I CAN *DIRECT* THAT ENERGY UPWARD... UPWARD...

...UNTIL IT STRIKES THE SPEEDING MISSILE, CAUSING IT TO CHANGE DIRECTION...TO FALTER...TO LOSE ALTITUDE!

Kirby
This first issue was drawn by legendary comic book artist Jack Kirby. Over the years, the style of X-Men art changed many times.

39

RUN! THE TANK IS MOVING BY *ITSELF!* GANGWAY!

IT..IT'S *IMPOSSIBLE!* AND YET...IT'S ACTING LIKE IT HAS A MIND OF ITS OWN! LIKE IT'S *TRYING* TO MENACE US!

SWISH!

CLANK!

CLANK!

Leapin' lizards
Magneto is not the only evil mutant the X-Men have battled. Others include Toad, who has superhuman leaping ability.

Machine guns and tanks spun out of control. They seemed to fire under their own power.

Finally, Magneto revealed himself— and his demands.

By magnetizing dust particles in the air, he created a grim message in the sky.

"SURRENDER THE BASE OR I'LL TAKE IT BY FORCE!"

Then he signed it...Magneto.

"Who or what is Magneto?" the general wondered.

As if in answer to the general's question, Magneto appeared. Creating a magnetic force field around himself, he walked through the base, repelling soldiers and weapons.

Magneto took over the base, sealing himself inside a huge force field that covered the entire facility.

At his School for Gifted Youngsters, Professor X listened with concern to radio reports of the crisis at Cape Citadel. He sent out a telepathic message which registered as a sharp command in the mind of each of the X-Men.

Attention, X-Men. Report to my study immediately!

When the team of five young heroes assembled, Professor X explained their mission.

"The first of the evil mutants has made his appearance. You must go to Cape Citadel and defeat him!"

Conventional weapons are powerless against Magneto's force field.

Super senses
Sabretooth has superhuman senses and fast healing ability. His powers are similar to those of Wolverine. The two have fought many epic battles.

BUT, THE ADDITIONAL REINFORCEMENTS ARE EQUALLY POWERLESS TO STOP THE ONE-MAN INVASION OF THE STRATEGIC BASE!

IT..IT'S LIKE HE'S GOT AN INVISIBLE *BARRIER* 'ROUND HIM, HURLING US AWAY..

The X-Men sprang into action. Arriving at the missile base, they approached Magneto's force field. Angel spread his wings and flew. Beast leaped over a group of soldiers. Marvel Girl telekinetically pushed soldiers out of her path.

When Cyclops reached the force field, Professor X contacted him telepathically. *Use your most powerful energy beam*, he instructed.

Shape changer
Other evil mutants the X-Men have battled include Mystique, who is a shape shifter. She can change her appearance to make herself look like anyone else.

I'M GETTING THROUGH! THAT'S WHAT WAS NEEDED A NATURAL COUNTERFORCE TO BATTER THE UNNATURAL MAGNETIC FIELD!

Cyclops fired his optic blast. The beam pushed through the force field and knocked Magneto to the ground.

"Another mutant is attacking me!" Magneto cried in shock. "I was unprepared. That will not happen again."

The X-Men burst through the open shield. *Look sharp, X-Men*, Professor X said telepathically. *You are facing a dangerous enemy!*

In retaliation, Magneto fired the base's heat-seeking missiles at the X-Men!

The missiles zoomed toward Angel. "Got to dodge them," he cried, flying out of the way. But the missiles gained on the winged X-Man.

Then Iceman flung his ice grenades.

Warmonger
Evil Apocalypse wants all-out war between humans and mutants.

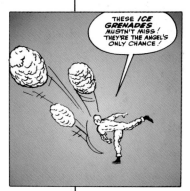

THESE *ICE GRENADES* MUSTN'T MISS! THEY'RE THE ANGEL'S ONLY CHANCE!

Fire!
Scarlet Witch can cause metal to melt or objects to burst suddenly into flames. She was once on the side of her father, Magneto, but now fights against evil mutants.

The ice grenades stopped the missiles...all but one!

Beast swung out from a ledge and caught the final missile with his huge feet. Then Marvel Girl telekinetically hurled it into the sea.

"Not all those with mutant powers are fit to rule the Earth!" Magneto shouted at the X-Men.

"You must be destroyed!"

Magneto sent a flaming tank of fuel toward the heroes.

"Get behind my shield!" Iceman cried, forming a protective ice shield.

BLAM! The fuel tank exploded. When the smoke cleared, the X-Men were nowhere to be seen.

"Now nothing will stand in my way!" Magneto shouted.

Suddenly the X-Men burst from the ground.

"Cyclops created a tunnel for us under the blast... saving us from the impact!" Angel explained. "And *now...*"

But Magneto was gone, propelling himself away from the base using his power of magnetic repulsion.

The X-Men had won their first battle, but they knew they would face Magneto another day.

Well done, X-Men, Professor X congratulated the heroes telepathically.

IT MEANS YOUR *FINISH*, MAGNETO!

CYCLOPS CREATED A TUNNEL FOR US UNDER THE BLAST WITH HIS ENERGY BEAM... SAVING US FROM THE IMPACT! AND *NOW...*

Swift! Quicksilver has the superhuman ability to think and move at incredible speeds.

The uncanny X-Men

Over the years, many mutants have joined the X-Men. The doors of Professor X's School for Gifted Youngsters are always open to mutants looking to learn how to control and develop their unique and astounding abilities.

In fact, some of the X-Men's former enemies, those who started as evil mutants, have since become allies of Professor X.

Quicksilver and Scarlet Witch both changed their evil ways and joined the Super Hero team, the Avengers.

The X-Men Rogue, Gambit, and Banshee all started out as evil mutants.

Gen X
Generation X is the newest team of X-Men. Its members include youngsters M, Chamber, Husk, Skin, Penance, Jubilee, and Synch, and teachers White Queen and Banshee.

The current generation of X-Men.

Magneto himself briefly became the leader of the X-Men before returning to his beliefs of mutant domination.

Even Emma Frost, the White Queen, who is now the leader of Generation X, started as an evil mutant. In time, Professor X hopes that all mutants, and all humans, will come to embrace his philosophy of mutants and humans living together in peace.

Fireworks
One of the most popular members of Generation X is Jubilee. She has the mutant power to shoot energy blasts from her fingers.

Glossary

Agility
The ability to move quickly and precisely.

Altitude
Height above sea level.

Amnesia
A condition where a person loses his or her memory.

Assemble
To gather or put together.

Biochemisty
The study of chemical reactions in living creatures.

Brutally
Cruelly, with the intention of hurting.

Debating
Two or more people discussing a subject on which they have different points of view.

Domination
Total control over a person or group of people.

Dormitory
A building where students live on the campus of a school.

Endurance
The ability to do physical activity for a long time without getting tired.

Fugitive
Someone who is running away from others.

Genetic
Having to do with the makeup of a person's genes, the coded information that makes each person unique.

Magnetism
An invisible force, produced by magnets or electricity, which has the power to move objects.

Oppression
To keep people down, in bad conditions, by the unjust use of power or force.

Outcast
Someone that has been pushed out of society.

Paralyze
To leave someone unable to move.

Philosophy
A belief that guides the way a person lives his or her life.

Recruit
To actively encourage someone to join a group.

Repelling
Sending away with great force.

Repulses
Sends away with great force.

Retaliation
The act of getting back at somebody for a wrong done by that person.

Shunned
Rejected or turned away.

Strategist
Someone who is good at making plans of action.

Telekinetic
Having the ability to move objects by the mind alone.

Telepath
Someone who can read the minds of other people.

Teleport
To vanish from one place and instantly reappear in another place, some distance away.

Terrorist
Someone who commits acts of violence for political reasons.

Toxic
Poisonous.

Withdrawn
Shy, quiet, not talking to other people.

Index

They're stars of comic books,
television, and a major movie.
Learn how the uncanny
X-Men got their start!

DK READERS

Stunning photographs combine with lively
illustrations and engaging, age-appropriate stories in
DK READERS, a multilevel reading program guaranteed
to capture children's interest while developing
their reading skills and general knowledge.

1 BEGINNING TO READ	Beginning to read	• Word repetition, limited vocabulary, and simple sentences • Picture dictionary boxes
2 BEGINNING TO READ ALONE	Beginning to read alone	• Longer sentences and increased vocabulary • Information boxes and alphabetical glossary • Simple index
3 READING ALONE	Reading alone	• More complex sentence structure • Information boxes and alphabetical glossary • Comprehensive index
4 PROFICIENT READERS	Proficient readers	• Rich vocabulary and challenging sentence structur • Additional information and alphabetical glossary • Comprehensive index

With DK READERS,
children will learn to read –
then read to learn!

ISBN 978-0-7894-6697-6

Discover more at
www.dk.com

9 780789 466976

detection